a

ZIMBABWE

Limpopo River

Matangari
Thohoyandou

MOZAMBIQUE

Pietersburg

Northern Province

Kruger National Park

Sun City

Mafikeng

Gauteng

Mpumalanga

Nelspruit

est

Pretoria
Johannesburg
Soweto
Evaton
Vereeniging
Sasolburg
Koppies

Swazi-
land

Kroonstad

al River

Free State

KwaZulu-
Natal

erley

Bloemfontein

Ulundi

Lesotho

Balito
Hammersdale
Durban

Eastern Cape

Indian
Ocean

Bisho

rahamstown

■ Provincial capitals   ○ Home towns

The story of my life

South Africa seen through the eyes of its children

Kwela Books

Compiled by **Han Lans**

This is a copublication of Kwela Books, Cape Town,
and KIT Publishers, Amsterdam.

Copyright © 2002 Han Lans

Kwela Books
28 Wale Street, Cape Town 8001;
P.O. Box 6525, Roggebaai 8012

Cover photographs by Han Lans
Cover design and typography by Michael
Stallenberg at Interactive Africa
Map of South Africa by Louw Venter
Set in Candida
Lithography by T & P Far East Productions
DTP by Grafisch Ontwerpbureau Agaatsz BNO
Printed and bound by
Delotiskarna, Slovenia
First edition, first printing 2002

ISBN 0-7957-0138-1

Contents

'For it is only by getting to know each other that we can create respect...'

FOReWord

by Nelson Mandela

It is a truth that children can communicate with each other, even if they can't speak each other's language. The challenge is to draw together children from different backgrounds so that they can use this gift to get to know each other. Only then will different groups of people grow up knowing how much they have in common, while at the same time appreciating what is different and unique about each other. For it is only by getting to know each other that we can create respect for each other's similarities and differences and live together in peace.

Unfortunately there are serious inequalities between the situation in which different children and groups of children find themselves. And this keeps people apart. Some children enjoy a privileged life and good education, while others suffer problems such as poverty, illiteracy, HIV/AIDS and other illnesses.

This lovely book is an example of how sharing information can advance understanding. In it the talents of twelve very different young South Africans are displayed. Whether they come from humble backgrounds or live in comfort, each child has clearly taken pride in what is his or hers. May everyone, child and adult alike, who views this book, work for a better future for all our children.

NELSON MANDELA

'**I wish**
all politicians could visit my school and see how
culture, colour & religion blind
we are ...'

NEELA BAMBERGER

About this book

Three years ago my son and I returned to Holland from a visit to South Africa. Yannick was eleven. It was his first visit and for school he wrote a report of his experiences. After visiting Kayelitsha and Gugulethu, two sprawling townships outside Cape Town, he wrote in his diary: 'I found the houses sad and poor, but the people were not. They were extremely friendly and cheerful.' It was a source of amazement to him.

After exploring the country a number of times on photographic commissions I, too, had become intrigued by the positive attitude of so many South Africans, especially of the black population who had suffered the effects of the apartheid policies.

How was it possible for people from so many different cultures, each with his or her own home language and sometimes of a different faith, to live peacefully together in one country, despite the hardship, the huge differences in income and material circumstances, I asked myself.

I wanted to find the answer by finding out what the children of South Africa made of their own lives and future. I knew that children would give the most honest and open answer.

With the help of Annari van der Merwe of Kwela Books in Cape Town, we found twelve children between the ages of ten and thirteen, from different parts of the country, different cultural groups, belonging to different religions and to seven of the eleven official language groups in the country. In each case somebody in the community, either a teacher or family friend, selected the particular child. Once contact was established, I visited each child in her or his home, gave each a camera and film and some instructions on how to take good photographs. I explained that we wanted them to do a 'reportage' of their own daily lives. They had to keep a diary and note down what they photographed.

Tendani, Nkosana, Neela, Bukekile, Inge, Mohau, Fernando, Umir, Natasha, Warren, Avanthi and Mlungesi had about three months to record their lives at home, at school, with family, friends and on holiday (if their families could afford it). The Easter holidays fell in this period. All the photographs inside the book are used in the way they were taken by the children. All captions were written by them, as well as the short pieces on themselves, their families and schools. Annari van der Merwe is responsible for the brief description of the region or town where each child lives which precedes the various stories.

I tried to visit all of the children a second time to collect the material and to talk to them about their everyday lives and dreams for the future. Together we have made a wonderful book which gives an unexpectedly telling insight into each child's world, culture, language and religion; his or her own values, likes and dislikes, dreams.

I trust that this book will not only show how different cultures coexist peacefully in South Africa, but also create, through the contribution of each of the children, a deeper understanding of their specific environment and culture, and through the understanding a genuine respect.

May you enjoy reading the book as much as we enjoyed making it. I'd like to conclude with Neela's words: 'I wish all politicians could visit my school and see how culture, colour and religion blind we are ...'

Han Lans
Amsterdam

AbOut South Africa's past

According to some paleontologists Africa is considered to be the cradle of humankind. The first people developed in Africa millions and millions of years ago and later many humans migrated from Africa and settled throughout the world. The existing written accounts of contact between Europe and Africa date from the 15th century. At that time Southern Africa was inhabited by various groups of people. Firstly, the San, a nomadic Stone Age people who lived very close to nature and who moved around hunting and gathering food from the wild. All over Southern Africa they left paintings and engravings in caves and on rocks. Secondly, the Khoikhoi, who were herders and followed a more settled lifestyle, and thirdly, the Iron Age, Bantu-speaking groups, who had migrated southward from Central Africa. The Venda, who belonged to this third group, settled in the Limpopo Valley on the northern border of South Africa.

The Tswana people settled in the dry, central part of Southern Africa. A group, which in the 19th century became Zulus, settled on the fertile east coast. The Xhosas went even further south and in the 17th century met up with people of European descent who had migrated northwards from the Cape of Good Hope.

In 1652 the Dutchman Jan van Riebeeck started a settlement at the Cape of Good Hope (known as Cape Town today). Because he was working for a private company, the Dutch East India Company (VOIC), he could not establish a colony. His duty was to start a refreshment station only and to supply the ships sailing between Europe and the East with fresh vegetables and meat.

At the Cape, the Dutch met the Khoikhoi people who had lived in the western and southern part of Southern Africa for many centuries. As herders, they could provide the fresh meat for the ships and to the Dutch settlement. The settlement at the Cape grew and the white farmers slowly started to move northwards with their live stock, the sheep and cattle they bartered from the Khoikhoi.

The Dutch were in command at the Cape for 150 years. In this time many foreign people arrived and stayed. But two groups of people in particular were important: the skilled Muslim slaves – tailors and builders and carpenters – with the political exiles whom the Dutch brought from Indonesia to help develop the Cape, and the French Huguenots who fled from France to escape being persecuted for their Protestant religion.

The British started governing the Cape in 1806. They changed the name to the Cape Colony. They quickly expanded into Southern Africa, because they were powerful, and like all the European powers, wanted a part of Africa. In 1820 the British Settlers arrived and were sent to the eastern border where there were already Dutch-speaking and Xhosa farmers. The farmers of Dutch descent, now called Boers, showed their dissatisfaction by starting the Great Trek north. The Xhosas fought the English like they fought the Boers, because they wanted to protect their grazing.

To get away from the British, the Boers went as far as what is now known as KwaZulu-Natal, but the land was already inhabited, so battles broke out between them and the Zulus. The Boers could in any case not get away from the British, because they had already established a presence in Natal. So the Boers left and went back inland and created two Boer republics: the Orange Free State and the Zuid-Afrikaansche Republiek (ZAR).

The black people who had previously lived in these areas had had to abandon their land, as a result of a series of wars which had broken out between the mighty Zulu forces and the other black groups. At this time the Basotho nation was also formed, because various groups of people took refuge from Shaka, the Zulu king, in the mountains of Lesotho. King Moshoeshoe was their wise and kind founder.

After some fierce battles in which the Zulus were beaten by the British, the Colony of Natal was established. The British now had two colonies in South Africa: the Cape and Natal. The Natal climate was good for growing sugarcane, so the British recruited people from India to work on the sugarcane fields. In this way many Indians settled in Natal.

In the meantime the British became interested in the two Boer republics, because diamonds were discovered in the Orange Free State and gold in the ZAR. In the end, the fight over these riches led to the Anglo-Boer War (or

but in 1948 the Nationalist government entrenched a policy by which only some South Africans were free: apartheid. Only the whites could vote, work and live where they wanted to. According to the government's policy of 'separate development' South Africans were divided into four ethnic groups: Whites, Coloureds, Asians and Africans. Different 'homelands' were created for the different black ethnic groups. Some became independent, others not.

After a long period of resistance and an armed struggle, during which many people lost their lives and many were imprisoned, South Africa became a democracy in which all are equal.

has eleven official languages. The Nguni languages – isiXhosa, isiZulu, isiNdebele and siSwati, the Sotho languages – Sesotho, Setswana and Sepedi, Tshivenda and Xitsonga are all recognised, but English is the main language of communication.

Religious toleration is an integral part of the new South African constitution. There are four major faiths in South Africa: Christianity, Islam, Judaism and Hinduism. The European settlers – the Dutch, the French, the English and the Boers – established the Christian faith wherever they went in Southern Africa. The spread of the Christian faith was strengthened and speeded up by various

After a long period of resistance and an armed struggle, South Africa became a democracy in which all are **equal.**

South African War, as it is also called), between the Boer forces and the mighty British Army. The Boers were defeated, and the British became the rulers of the whole of South Africa.

In 1910 the Union of South Africa was formed, with the following provinces: Cape Province, Orange Free State, Transvaal and Natal. South Africa now held the position of a Dominion in the British Empire.

In 1961 the Republic of South Africa was established. The country was now completely independent from Britain,

The first democratic elections took place in 1994 and Nelson Mandela was elected president. The four former provinces were divided into nine new provinces: Transvaal disappeared and Gauteng, Northwest, the Northern Province and Mpumalanga were created. The Cape Province was divided into the Western Cape, Northen Cape and Eastern Cape. The Orange Free State became the Free State and Natal became KwaZulu-Natal.

Instead of two official languages, English and Afrikaans, South Africa now

missionary societies who created mission stations among the indigenous peoples. The Muslim faith came to the Cape with the political exiles and slaves whom the Dutch brought from the East, and the Hindu faith arrived in the country with the Indian immigrants brought to KwaZulu-Natal by the British. Judaism was the faith of the Jewish immigrants who made South Africa their home.

photo: Fernando Luwango

The story of my life

Tendani Makwarela

The closest big town to Matangari village is Thohoyandou, called after the man who created the Venda nation more than 200 years ago. The name means 'Head of the Elephant'.

Thohoyandou used to be the capital of Venda, the 'homeland' of the Venda people. Since 1994, Venda is part of the Northern Province.

The Vendas trace their origins back to about a thousand years ago. In those days their ancestors lived around the Limpopo. This river forms the border between South Africa and Zimbabwe. The Venda lang- uage is unlike other African languages. The culture is also unique. Many people in this area still follow the old Venda traditions and beliefs, and some elders like to tell the ancient tales and legends they heard as children.

Matangari is very close to South Africa's northern bor- der. It is only about 20 km from the famous Kruger National Park. Each year thousands of tourists visit this game reserve to view lions, leopards, elephants, rhinoceros and other wildlife from the safety of their vehicles. The thing that can do them

most harm is an insect – the malaria-carrying mosquito!

On some privately-owned game farms nearby, people can pay to hunt animals. But hunting is very expensive and is allowed only at certain times of the year.

Because of the subtropical climate, fruits like pawpaws, bananas, avocados and mangos grow wild in the Northern Province. Oranges are also grown for the export market.

The capital of the Northern Province is Pietersburg. Tshivenda is not the only language spoken in the province. People also speak Xitsonga or Sepedi or Afrikaans or English at home.

TeNdani

I was born on 19 April 1989 at William Eddie Clinic in the Venda area of the Northern Province. My birth caused great excitement. My grandfather even came all the way from Pretoria to see me because I was his first granddaughter.

I like watching TV and reading stories. Sometimes I like going out for picnics or visiting relatives.

My best friend is Vusani. She is my neigh- bour. We go to school together. We play together.

We attend the same church. We also make the Sunday school trip together.

My biggest wish is to become a doctor. I want to cure people who are suffering from different kinds of diseases. I also want to invent a medicine that can cure HIV/AIDS which is killing people in multiple numbers.

I am afraid of snakes. My fear became worse when I saw a certain gentlemen on the TV with a swollen leg because of a snake bite.

13

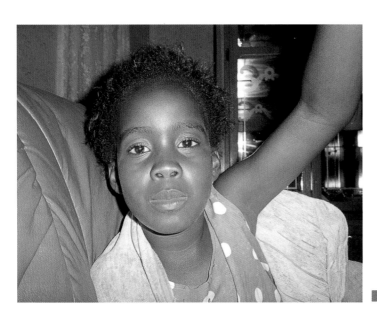

■ This is where I live.

■ My brother Mpfunzeni,
my sister Rendani and myself
in our living room, watching TV.

■ Rendani is seven years
old and a very happy child.

My family

My family has six members. I live with my father, mother, brother and sister and cousin. We have been living in this house for six years. We moved here during December 1995. My cousin came from her village and joined us in February 2000, when the bridge between her house and the school was washed away.

Our house has got seven rooms and one garage. I share my room with my cousin and my sister Rendani. We take turns to clean the room.

The name of my father is Saul and my mother's name is Leah. My father is a teacher, like my mother. They teach at different primary schools. The name of my brother is Mpfunzeni. He is so funny.

My grandparents live in the same village where we live. They are all pensioners. They love us very much. Whenever they get their monthly grant, they buy chicken for us. I love them very much.

■ My mother does not work during the weekend. Here she is sitting in our garden under a mango tree.

■ Rendani crying in the passage. We do not have doors inside our house.

■ My cousin Princess stays with us because she can't go to school from her own house because the bridge was washed away.

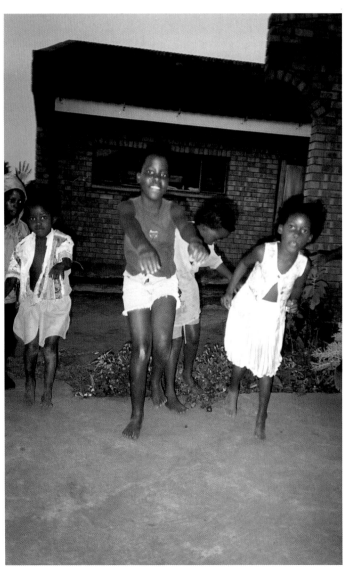

■ I put the camera on a table and took a picture of myself in the study room.

■ My friend Salome on the pit toilet in our back yard. We do not have flush toilets.

■ My friends dancing on my twelfth birthday.

■ We mostly play outside. Here we are skipping with a rope.

■ My friends playing with their cars made of wire.

■ My friends hanging like mangos from the mango tree. We don't have to buy fruit, we can pick any fruit from any tree around us – mangos, bananas, oranges, pawpaws, avocados.

■ On our way to school we walk through the fields.

■ In the morning we start our school day with an assembly at quarter past seven.

■ During first break some ladies come to sell biscuits and sweets at school. During second break we have a proper meal.

My school

The name of my school is Ndidivhani. It starts at quarter to eight in the morning in winter and quarter past seven in summer. Each year we have a school trip. The name of our principal is Mr Ramano. We have fun activities in our school. In the afternoons we play netball and football. My school ends at quarter to two in winter and five past one in summer.

We have two breaks at our school. The short break is for going to the toilet and the long break is for eating food which is supplied by the government. We eat porridge and cabbage and bread and drink orange juice.

I like school because that is where I get an education to build my life on. The school is an interesting place because you meet other kids there and compete in class.

■ My classmates in Grade 6. There are 33 children in my class and we have about 340 children in our school.

■ Tshilidzi and Avhapfani have just come home from school. They live in a traditional house called 'nndu'. The roof is thatched with banana leaves.

■ I also attend Sunday school. Here my friends are dancing for a fund-raising event.

■ Tendani, who shares my name, sweeping their yard. We keep our houses and yards very clean.

■ We all have to do some housework after school. My friend, who is also called Rendani, is pounding mealies. In my language we say 'mutuli na musi'.

■ These are famous Venda pots for keeping water, beer or sorghum. They care called 'mvuvhelo'.

■ My friend Vusani carrying a baby on her back in the traditional way.

■ This is an important tree. The 'muelela' is where the elders gather for meetings and the old people go to receive their pension money. It is our traditional meeting place.

■ We fetch our water from the river when the water supply has run out. It is a long way and we use wheelbarrows to carry the containers.

■ Malaria is a problem in our region. The truck regularly comes around to spray the houses with chemicals that kill the mosquitoes which carry the malaria virus.

■ These ladies at the Thohoyandou shopping centre are selling hair combs, sweets and mopani worms, a traditional dish.

■ Nkosana Roda

Mafikeng means 'Place of Stones'. On some rocky outcrops around the town one finds very old stone engravings. They tell us that for thousands of years the land was inhabited by the San people. Later on the Tswanas moved here and settled in a wide area which also includes Botswana.

Mafikeng is close to the Botswanan border. The town was founded in the 1880s by farmers and British mercenaries who received land from warring chiefs in return for helping them. A town was laid out on their land and the British started to use Mafikeng as an administrative centre.

During the Anglo-Boer (or South African) War the Siege of Mafeking made the town world-famous. The siege took place in 1899 and lasted seven months. During the siege, a small group of boys formed a cadet corps, carrying messages and helping around the town. Colonel Baden-Powell, who led the siege, was so inspired by this that he later founded the Scout move- ment. During the war the writer Sol Plaatje, the first General Secretary of the ANC, lived in Mafikeng. For three years he kept a diary which was later published as Sol Plaatje's Boer War Journals.

In the apartheid years a new city called Mmabatho ('Mother of the People') was built next to Mafikeng. It was built as the capital of the independent 'homeland' of Bophuthatswana. A parliament and other government buildings were erected. Also a university and some big shopping centres. In 1994 Bophuthatswana became part of South Africa again and the town was again called by its original name. Now some people talk of Mafikeng - Mmabatho. It is the capital of the Northwest Province.

Nkosana

I was born on 28 August 1989 at Victoria Hospital in Mafikeng. On the same day my father organised a great concert that was a big success!

I have lived in Mafikeng all my life. It is a historic place, but it can get quite boring because it is a small town and sometimes not much happens here.

My house is not that big. It has seven rooms. My room is always messy. It is only clean when my sister is at home. It is a big room with many pictures on the walls.

I like watching TV but I like going to movies with friends, or just talking to them, more. I really dislike it when people don't get along and turn to violence. I also dislike cruelty to animals.

I want to be a cricket player and I want to become a businessman, because I have good ideas on how to make money.

23

■ My house in Mafikeng. It has seven rooms.

■ This is my mother. She likes to shout at me a lot, but she is the most important person in my life because I live with her and she is the one who makes sure I look perfect for school every day.

■ My sister Thenjiwe. She is eight years older than me and studies Law in Johannesburg.

■ When my sister is in Mafikeng she likes to talk on the phone with her friend Doris who lives in Johannesburg.

My family

I have one sister. Her name is Thenjiwe and she lives in Johannesburg. She is studying Law and is in her second year of study. She is eight years older than me, therefore there are very few things we fight about, except over who should control the TV.

My father is a impresario and has a company by the name of Morris Roda Productions. He has brought people like Michael Jackson and Whitney Houston to South Africa. My father is based in Johannesburg.

My mom is a bank official at Standard Bank in Mafikeng. Her job is very interesting. I am left with only one grandma, my mom's mother, who lives in Evaton, near Vereeniging.

My biggest wish is to always have the people I love close to me. My worst fear is being without either my parents and sister for any reason.

■ Our maid, whom we lovingly call 'Ousie', which means 'maid or 'sister', loves to clean our house. She lives about 10 km from our house and she comes in twice a week.

■ I am trying my best to be a cool dude.

■ My mom works at Standard Bank in Mafikeng, six days a week. She is a financial adviser. Here she is with a colleague.

■ My father Morris. He is a promoter for big-time artists like Michael Jackson and Whitney Houston. He always wants to look clean so he washes twice a day.

■ Ma'mpho, my cousin, in my dad's living room in Johannesburg.

■ My sister leaving her university flat in Johannesburg and coming home to Mafi-keng with her friend Thandi.

■ My mother's mother, Granny Elizabeth, is very good at making crocheted table clothes and sewing.

■ My grandma always goes to church on Sundays. It is a Methodist Church and it is 1 km from her home.

■ My grandma lives about 400 km from us in Evaton. She does not want to leave this house because she has been living here for 20 years.

■ Kabelo, a great soccer player, in front of my school, the International School of South Africa, in Mafikeng.

■ My friends Nomdeni from Mafikeng and Kelly from Nelspruit in Mpumalanga. They love colouring in and going to the movies. Here they are in our classroom.

■ We had Entrepeneurship lessons. We learn how to make a living advertising and selling. I love selling hotdogs, sweets and chips. Both Grade 6 classes were in one classroom. During Entrepeneurship lessons we are all taught in one classroom.

My school

I attend the International School of South Africa, a private school in Mafikeng. The school has classes from pre-primary right through to A-levels. We follow the British school system.

There are about 40 teachers on the staff and there are just over 600 pupils. The subjects taught are English, Mathematics, Integrated Studies, IT, Gym, Music and Art. The pupils come from all over Africa and some other places like England, Germany, the USA and Denmark. Those who come from far stay in boarding houses.

In the afternoons there are sporting activities like cricket, basketball, soccer, tennis, netball, hockey, swimming and clubs for chess, wild life and French. I play cricket for the school under-13 team. I am a very good all-rounder.

My best friend is Laurent who also lives in Mafikeng. We are best friends because we trust each other. We do many things together, like going to the movies, playing cricket and we sometimes also do our homework together.

■ The principal handed out stickers to our teachers to praise and thank them for their good work. On the right is my Grade 6 teacher, Mr Everson.

■ With this kombi I go to school and back home, together with the other learners who don't stay in the boarding-houses but with their families.

■ The last day of the school term, ready to go home.

■ My cousins Thato and Kagiso who live in Gauteng enjoy cooking.

■ This is where I buy my sweets in Mondeor. I like them, but in Johannesburg you can buy nicer sweets. I go to Johannesburg to visit my father during every school holiday.

■ Tebogo, a family friend, at the family braai. I like pap and wors, which we often eat at braais.

My cute cousin Thato was cold so she decided to wear her traditional Basotho blanket. She then decided to wear the traditional Basotho hat as well.

This is KB, short for Kabelo. He is showing off with his winning Monopoly cards at his home in Mafikeng.

My two cousins Mmabatho and Boitumelo like doing each other's hair. They live in Johannesburg.

My friend Thulane likes to play with toy guns, but mostly he likes to be cool.

Neela Bamberger

The name Gauteng was given to the richest and smallest province of South Africa in 1994. But for many, many years already, 'Gauteng' was the name by which Johannesburg was known to Sotho-speaking people. Nguni-speakers called Johannesburg 'eGoli'. Both names mean 'Place of Gold'. It is a fitting name, because gold was discovered here on the Witwatersrand in 1885 and soon afterwards people from all over Southern Africa and the rest of the world started flocking to Johannesburg. They came to the 'Place of Gold' to find work on the mines or to start businesses. Many people living and working in Johannesburg today therefore trace their roots to other parts of the world: Germany, Greece, Great Britain, France, India, Israel, Italy, the Netherlands, Portugal, Russia and many, many more.

Johannesburg is the biggest and most industrialised city in South Africa. It is the financial capital, not only of South Africa, but also of the whole of Southern Africa. The Johannesburg Stock Exchange is here and branch offices of many foreign banks. Most international airlines fly only as far as Johannesburg, from where passengers continue their journey to other destinations.

There is another important city in Gauteng: Pretoria, the administrative capital of the country. It is here, in the Union Buildings, that the President and his Cabinet have their offices and where they can be found in the second half of the year when Parliament is not sitting in Cape Town. Johannesburg and Pretoria are 55 km apart.

NeELa

I was born on 17 November 1989 at the Park Lane Clinic in Parktown, Johannesburg. I am told I came out smiling, pink, fat and gorgeous, with a curl on the top of my head. I live in Greenside, Johannesburg.

I just love to dance. When I'm dancing I feel happy. I do ballet four times a week and Irish and Highland dancing twice a week. We often have Irish and Highland competitions on the weekends all over the place. I am going to enter the Concor, the big ballet competition, at the end of this year, so I've started working very hard on my individual dance. In my spare time I like making all sorts of beaded jewellery, which I'm supposed to sell to earn pocket money, but I often land up giving them to my friends.

■ We have a beautiful house in Greenside, Johannesburg. It is quite big. We all have our own bedrooms. We have a big garden to play and have fun in and recently got a swimming pool which is a total blast!

■ My brother Noah in our kitchen, talking to my dad. He is very energetic and seldom quiet.

■ At the weekend you can always find my parents chit-chatting on the front steps of our house with friends. My father used to sell juggling balls with the red scooter car parked near the fence.

My family

I'm eleven and a half and my brother, Noah, is eight.

My dad's parents came from Germany and Russia and my mom's parents from Russia and Israel. I am Jewish, a mixture between Ashkenazi and Safardic. My parents were both born in South Africa. My brother and I too. We are all very similar and very different people. I think we all have a love for life and enjoy what we do and we all do something special.

My dad makes very interesting couches and furniture. He also plays the piano and bakes great cakes. My mom can make pots, cooks delicious food and makes sure that everybody is happy. In the mornings she works at my grandfather's antique shop. My mom's parents are divorced.

My mom and dad love dancing and they go for ballroom dancing lessons on Tuesdays. Noah loves to swim in summer and to play soccer in winter. He plays chess whenever he can find an opponent. He also does karate, trades in Poké-mon cards and watches TV.

■ This is my mom – organising transport, making arrangements: I've got ballet, my brother has soccer, and Dad's hungry. He wants lunch.

■ Maisie, who looks after us on a Tuesday evening when my mom and dad have dancing lessons. Maisie has been living with us for eight years since Noah was born.

■ My parents like cooking and we spend a lot of time in the kitchen. My dad bakes great cakes and my mom cooks delicious pastas.

■ My Grandpa Gideon playing chess with Noah. Noah loves chess and I think he has beaten Grandpa most of the times they play. He is my favourite grandpa.

■ Saturdays are great fun. People pop in and out for tea. My parents have a lot of funny friends, such as Tony Bentel the architect who used to be a ballet dancer, and Lawly, a lawyer.

■ While the grown-ups were having late tea, Lawly Shein's children and Noah got up to mischief and made a nice fire in the driveway.

■ We often go on to the roof of Maisie's room for quiet time and the best part is you can see all over the garden and the neighbourhood. This is my fun picture of Alice and Jo who are identical twins and two of my best friends.

■ The view from the roof of Maisie's room, which is at the back of the house.

■ I also love dancing, but not the same kind as Mom and Dad. After school I practise ballet as well as Irish and Highland dancing.

■ At my school we have big sports grounds where we can play netball, cricket, soccer, hockey, stingers and so on and so on. Here I am with some of my friends from Grade 6.

■ Gugu's gang waiting in the school grounds for the taxi to take them back to Soweto. It's a long wait but it's worth it to come all the way to Emmarentia Primary. In the meantime they are playing a good game of netball.

■ Gugu caught catching the netball.

My school

My school's name is Emmarentia Primary School. It's just up the road from where we live in Greenside.

My school is a government school and there are kids from all over who come every day. Some come from around the area we live in and some come from as far as Soweto and Alexandra Township. It is a great mix of cultures and religions. We have Christian, Jewish, Muslim and Hindu kids, as well as kids speaking all nine black official languages.

My principal, Mrs Steyn, is very strict, but we all love her very much. She keeps everybody at school in their place and she seems to always know exactly what's going on.

My teachers this year are all great, especially Mrs Gordon. She has a lovely personality. She's inspired me to improve my English and to play netball. She's my coach.

■ We're doing our best to learn Zulu, a language spoken by some of the children at school. But it is not easy and we do a lot of oral exercises and short plays.

■ Two bright sparks hard at work in the Guidance class where we learn about human values and different religions.

■ A portrait taken of my friend Fulu, short for Fulufela, during Mrs Vonk's Afrikaans class. Fulu speaks Tswana at home. She is extremely weird and that's what I like about her.

■ We went on a family picnic near Magaliesberg with my mother's mother, Grandma Bea. Grandma is sitting to my left; Noah, quiet for one second, is sitting between me and Mom.

■ Noah going flat out on a go-cart at Magaliesberg. He is a natural racing driver.

■ Every second Friday we have supper and say prayers during Sabbath at my grandfather's house. My mother's family is more traditional than my father's. That is why we observe the Sabbath at Grandpa Gideon's place.

■ During the Easter holidays I went to Cape Town all by myself to visit our good friends the Weebers in Hout Bay. My friends Amy and Shan jumping on the trampoline in the garden. The Weebers built their house themselves.

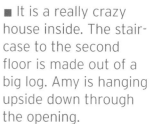

■ It is a really crazy house inside. The staircase to the second floor is made out of a big log. Amy is hanging upside down through the opening.

■ The Weeber kids are in the Zip Zap Children's Circus in Cape Town. So this is what circus kids do in their spare time!

■ The seawater around Cape Town is freezing cold because it comes straight from the Antarctic. It never gets warmer than 14 degrees. Shan and I are shivering on the beach at Fish Hoek.

■ Bukekile Banjwa

Soweto is the biggest black township in South Africa. It can be called Johannesburg's twin city. From the early 1950s it was developed exclusively for black people under the 'separate development' system of the apartheid regime. Many people living in Soweto today first lived in other parts of Johannesburg, but because they were black they had to move here.

The name Soweto is short for SOuth WEstern TOwnships and it includes 26 town areas, among them Diepkloof, Dube, Orlando, Meadowlands and Dobsonville. About two million people live in Soweto.

The inhabitants of Soweto speak many different languages – isiZulu, Sesotho, isiXhosa, Setswana, English, Tshivenda and some others – and include members of all the black ethnic groups in South Africa. People who speak isiZulu came from KwaZulu-Natal; those who speak Sesotho came from the Free State, the isiXhosa-speakers originally came

from the Eastern Cape, and so on. Most Sowetans still have relatives in the rural areas their parents and grandparents left when they first came to Gauteng. Because so many people still move to the cities to find work, there are not enough built houses for everyone. So some people put up their own structures, using wood and

corrugated iron, and live in informal settlements. In the informal settlements people usually do not have running water or electricity inside their houses.

Most of the people living in Soweto work in Johannesburg. They travel back and forth every day by bus and train and kombi taxis.

BuKekile

I was born at Barangwanath Hospital in Soweto in January 1989. I am the last-born at home. I like playing with my friends and sharing ideas with them, doing homework together and helping each other. Before there was electricity where I live, we used to play hide-and-seek outside in the evenings. It was very dark then and early in the morning we had to fetch water outside. I used to cry for my mother when she had to go out working.

I don't like arguing and fighting with people. My biggest wish is to help people who have diseases like HIV/AIDS. I want to fight this disease. People should stop hanging around and stop crime. I am afraid of rhinoceros and snakes and monkeys and cows and pigs.

■ My mother in front of where I live. Our house is made of corrugated iron. In Xhosa we call a shelter 'umzi'. My mother speaks Xhosa and my father speaks Zulu.

■ During the day my father is a delivery man. After hours he earns extra money by selling small bottles of perfume for R5 each. Here he fills them himself against the wall outside our house.

■ My big sister Thobeka lives in the second of the four shelters that form our house. She teaches at Thaba Jabula evening-school in Soweto.

My family

We live at Fred Clark squatter camp in south Soweto. A squatter camp is where there are no regular houses and no running water. My family lives in four shelters. They are three metres by three metres each. I sleep with my mother in one bed in the third small house. My grandparents, who used to live in a small village in the country, passed away.

I have three brothers and two sisters. My big brothers Zukile and Nkosiyezwe are both 22 years old and Sizwe, my younger brother, is 15.

My sister Thobeka is 27 and my small sister Bongiwe is 13. My two big brothers don't work. My big sister works as a teacher and my father works as a delivery man. My mother is an entrepreneur. She sells school socks, belts and washing towels. They all come home between six and seven at night.

At home I speak Xhosa but when I speak with my friends I speak Zulu, because if I speak Xhosa they don't understand me.

■ Two of my brothers, Sizwe, who is 15, and Nkosiyezwe, 22. They share the first shelter and are also very good friends. Sizwe is in high school and Nkosiyezwe is unemployed.

■ My mother having tea in front of the wood stove in the third shelter. Here we cook, watch TV, and my parents and I also sleep here. We only use the stove in the winter when it is cold. Otherwise we cook on two electric hotplates.

■ Every day when I come home from school I have to clean the house first, because my mom comes home late from work. Here I do the washing up at a friend's house.

■ Even Sizwe helps in the house, but he always wants to be paid!

■ Here Sizwe is repairing the electric hotplates because it costs money to have them fixed by someone else.

■ My big 'sisi' Buhle, my uncle's daughter, spends most of her time cleaning her house behind our shelter.

■ In Fred Clarke where I live, we do not have running water in our houses, so people wash their clothes outside in communal tubs.

■ Many mothers in Soweto are entrepreneurs with small businesses, just like my mother who sells socks and belts.

■ On my way to school we walk along Old Potchefstroom Road, which is the main road that runs right through Soweto.

■ The favourite sport for girls in our school is netball. We play against other schools in Soweto.

My school

The name of my school is Lakeview Primary. It is in Foxlake in Soweto. I am doing Grade 5. In my class we are 32 children and at school we are about 605. My school is not too far from my house, but when I go to school I walk for 25 minutes.

At school I speak many languages but my home language is Xhosa. Why do I speak many languages? Because I want other children to understand me when I speak to them.

I like going to school because I learn there so that I can be a doctor one day. I love to be educated.

■ We want to warn school children against the dangers of AIDS. That is why AIDS KILLS is written on the wall of the school.

■ Economics is my favourite subject. We have to answer our teacher giving us a questionnaire. We sit six to a table.

■ Girls and boys wear different uniforms to school. I am in Grade 7. Next year I'm going to high school.

■ Keke and Bobo, sitting on either side of another girl, are the two boys in my class I like best. We are a group of six best friends. Here they play with Pokémon cards.

Bongile is posing in front of a wall where everybody writes graffiti. The boy in front is Sello. He sings in my church choir although he loves beng cool.

Sipho made a car out of wire and tins. We have no street lights and I took this picture in the dark.

Nomphumelelo is my best friend. She also lives in Fred Clarke. I have known her for three years. We met at McDonald's in Southgate on my birthday. On Saturdays we often go to Southgate to play games.

■ On Mondays and Fridays after school Simangele and Khensane, two friends from school, and I teach some smaller children Zulu, Maths, Geography and English. They do go to school but they also come to our 'school' because they want to be educated like me.

■ In April they 'graduated'. We celebrated with frood and drinks. They each had to contribute R2 so we could be buy rice and chicken and chips.

■ We also did a traditional dance called 'umxhentso'.

■ I want to be educated like my sister Thobeka who graduated in Xhosa and Economics from Vista University in April this year. My mom, in a traditional Xhosa dress, and my aunt celebrated with her.

Inge Leonard

Kroonstad is called after a horse named 'Kroon' (Crown). This horse belonged to a Voortrekker, they say, and when it drowned in a pot-hole in a river, the man gave his name to the town which was started there in 1855. The Voortrekkers were descendants of the Dutch who came to the Cape of Good Hope (now the Western Cape) just over 200 years earlier. They did not like the new British rulers who took over governing the Cape, so they trekked north with all their belongings and created their own republic, the Orange Free State. The Afrikaners in the Free State are mostly the descendants of the Voortrekkers.

The Orange Free State was one of the two Boer republics which fought against the British in the Anglo-Boer (or South African) War to keep their independence. They lost, and in 1902 the Treaty of Vereeniging brought an end to the war.

Bloemfontein is the capital of the Free State, but Kroonstad is the most important town in the northern part of the province. It lies on the main route from Cape Town to Johannesburg, and has been a transportation centre since the early days. In those days the transport-riders with their heavily laden wagons stopped over in the town on their way to and from the goldfields of the Witwatersrand. Today goods transported by road and by rail still pass through the town. Because it is such a busy agricultural centre, tons of maize, wheat and sorghum are loaded from the huge grain elevators onto trucks and trains.

Kroonstad is also an education centre. Many farmers and farm-workers from the surrounding towns and farms bring or send their children to the various schools in town.

InGe

I was born on 17 December 1990 at two o'clock on the Monday afternoon. My grandpa, my mother's father, Piet Rademan, who is a doctor, delivered me. He delivered my two older sisters as well. He is 78 now.

I could play the piano since I was very small. At five I passed my first piano exam with honours - Grandma Olga taught me how to play and I was the youngest in the country. Now I no longer like to practise the piano. I also do not like school work very much. I prefer to play and eat.

My greatest wish is to own a mountain bike and take to the road. I'm not sure yet what I want to be when I am grown up. I like to take photos and I like people, especially children, but I really don't like sitting behind a desk. Perhaps I will become a pilot or a gladiator or something adventurous.

■ Our house at Kristalkop. We have been living here for 12 years. Before that my parents stayed on a farm near Sasolburg.

■ My mom and dad are very fond of each other. With them are Heléne and our two dogs, Note and Vivaldi.

■ We have a big garden on the farm and my little sister Heléne loves to play in it.

My family

I live with my mom and dad and little sister. We are four daughters. Olga, 16, is the oldest. She plays the piano and flute beautifully and also sings very well. She is clever and excels at school. Trudie, 14, is equally musically talented and clever. They are at boarding school in Pretoria to study the piano with a professor at the University of Pretoria. They only spend holidays and weekends at home.

My little sister Heléne spends all day, every day with my mom - they read books together, play the piano, sing, cycle and farm with my dad.

My dad is a farmer and he can make all sorts of plans. My mom is a professional mother - she sews and cooks well and is always there when we need her. She writes good speeches and is never late.

The size of our farm is 1 000 hectare.

■ My room on the farm where I do my homework. I share my room with Heléne.

■ My big sister Olga playing the piano. She is at boarding school in Pretoria and practises when she is home for the weekend.

■ There are two women who help my mother with the housework. Here is Maria, one of them, in the kitchen.

■ Our farm dam where rainwater is stored. The Free State often suffers droughts and such a dam is very valuable then.

■ When my dad and I drive around the farm we always look for the ostriches. We had to go very fast to take a photo of this one, because he can run up to 60 km per hour.

■ My dad grows maize, corn, sunflowers, groundnuts and feed sorghum. Soyabeans are harvested in May, June.

■ The maize crop is being loaded onto the back of a lorry. My dad also farms with cattle and sheep.

■ Olga in the back of the kombi on our way to Ballito on the KwaZulu-Natal north coast. This is where we spent our April school holidays this year.

■ While we were at Ballito, we visited Durban. We went to watch the dolphins in the Aquarium.

■ It is a great treat for Heléne to be on the beach.

■ We also strolled past many stalls selling handicrafts.

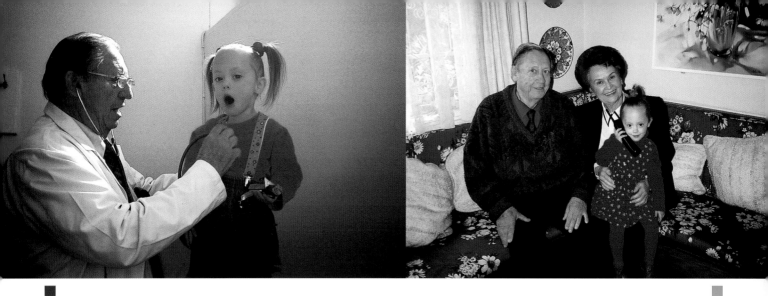

■ Grandpa Piet Rademan is widely known for the excellent diagnoses he makes and for the operations he performs – he took out my tonsils as well. Here he is listening Heléne's chest.

■ On Tuesdays I stay over with my grandparents in Kroonstad. They live near my school. In her young days Grandma Olga Rademan won an overseas study bursary with her organ performance and went to London. This is where she met my grandpa.

■ My little sister is tiny! She is three and weighs 11 kilogram and fits into a cool box. She weighed only 900 gram at birth, but now she is just fine.

■ Grandma Rademan invited over some of the family whom she doesn't often see. They lunched in her garden.

■ My two grannies are good friends and often visit each other. My dad's mother, Trudie Leonard, is an outstanding seamstress and cooks the nicest food and jams.

■ We go to church every Sunday. I like the holy atmosphere in our church and I'm pleased that we do not dance and clap hands in our church.

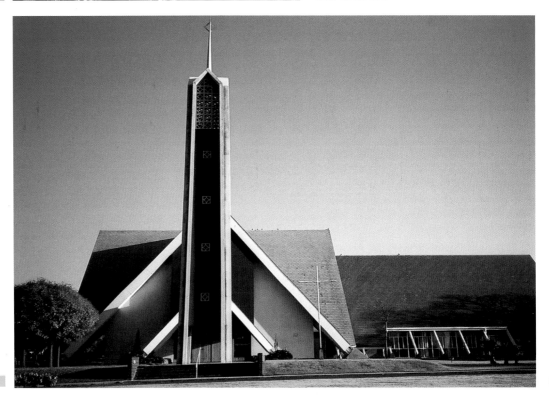

■ I usually go to school by bus, but sometimes my mom takes us by car. The bus takes 40 children. We catch it at twenty to seven in the morning. If you are late, you get left behind.

■ The Grade 6 girls eating their sandwiches during first break, from ten past to half past ten. Shorné Kraay stands at the back and Elani de Meyer, Juli Dykman, Louisa Uys en Janette van der Merwe are in front. They think they are the bee's knees.

■ During break the Grade 3 girls chase the boys and they tease one another. We always play barefoot.

My school

The name of my school is Kroonstad Akademie. It is a private school. There are 150 pupils. The oldest children are in Grade 10. The school should go up to Grade 12, but there are not enough pupils. We have 13 teachers. There are only six children in our class. Our school uniform is quite pretty.

We have assembly only on Mondays. On other mornings we just gather in the quad.

We do not practise sports during school hours. We do that in the afternoons. I can't participate because we live too far from the school. Each day I travel about 40 km to school by bus and back again to sleep at home each night.

I love break time at school, but I do not like to work and to study – my mom says I am a real 'los-gat' – a real happy-go-lucky!

■ I'm in Grade 5. There are only six pupils in my class, two girls and four boys: Heinrich Wiegand, Reinard Snyman, Thomas Kraay and A J Crause.

■ Colette, the other girl in my class, studies very hard. I prefer to kick ball with the boys and to run around.

■ My classmates Colette and Heinrich playing chess during school time.

■ Our parents must raise the funds themselves to keep our school going because it is a private school. This year they operated a food stall at the Bloemfontein Show to make some money. This is Stefan Erasmus, one of my school friends.

Mohau 'Director' Tshabalala

Kroonstad is an important farming district in the northern Free State. Before the days of farming thousands of springbok, blesbok and wildebeest used to roam the plains. But these animals were hunted for their meat and skins until very few were left. Today one sees only large fields of mealies, wheat, sunflower and sorghum – no antelope. Many farmers also have big herds of sheep and cattle, and produce wool, meat and dairy products.

Maize, or mealies, is South Africa's most important crop. Kroonstad is part of what is known as the 'maize triangle' because so much maize is produced here. The farms are usually very large. In this area crop-farming is completely mechanised and seeds are sown and crops harvested with big machines. But workers are still needed to use the machines. They usually live on the farms where they work. Some farmers have built farm-schools for the children of their workers who can't afford to send their children to town schools.

The farm-owners in the Free State mostly speak Afrikaans, while the farm workers mostly speak Sesotho. This is the language also spoken in Lesotho on the eastern border of the Free State. This is not a problem because usually the farm people are multi-lingual.

Lesotho is an independent kingdom and not part of South Africa. It got its independence from Great Britain in 1966. The Sotho nation came into being not so long ago. About 200 years ago many people sought shelter in the valleys and mountains of Lesotho. A young chief named Moshoeshoe gathered them together. This intelligent and kind leader gave them protection and in the end became the first Basotho king.

Mohau

I was born on 15 March 1988 in Johannesburg, but our home is now at Kristalkop, Mr Leonard's farm near Kroonstad. When I go to school I stay with my aunt because it is too far to walk to school from my parents' house.

I do not know my grandparents, I don't even know where they stayed.

I like playing soccer. It's a game I really enjoy a lot. I wish I could be like Thabo Mngomeni who plays for Orlando Pirates and like Jabu Pule who plays for Chiefs.

I also like school. I wish to be educated because when I'm grown-up I want to be somebody in society. I am educating myself so that I can become a doctor and heal people.

I am on the left in the picture above.

■ These are my brothers, Boy and Keki, in front of our yellow brick house at Kristalkop.

■ Ntate, as I call my father, works as a driver for Mr Leonard.

■ My mother, whom I call Mme, with my younger brother Mangaliso, relaxing in one of the rooms at home.

My family

I have four brothers and five sisters. Two of them are married. So altogether there are twelve of us. My father's name is Derick and my mother is called Mamohau. The rest of the family are my brothers Boy, Nkosana, Molukhisi, Botse and Mangaliso, and my sisters Nomalanga, Nose-khaya, Mamai, Mangaka, Qibi and Mashease. We speak Sesotho to each other.

One of my brothers and two of my sisters live in Johannesburg. They send us money at the end of every month. Life on the farm is not like life in Gauteng, thus my brothers and sisters left for Johannesburg to work there.

My father's job is to drive the tractors on the farm. He tills the mealie fields. My mother works in the Leonards' farmhouse, in the kitchen. Our house has three rooms.

■ Mangaliso, my younger brother.

■ Because the Free State is so flat and transport is so scarce, some people use bicycles. Our bike is kept inside the storage shack.

■ My brother's wife Mmokgo with my sister Mangaka and her daughter Mosele at our home. Mmokgo is wearing a Basotho blanket.

■ Our neighbours Paballo and Maroboko are watching TV at their house. Everybody would like to have a TV.

■ My friends Thabo, Maki, Tsumpa and Bongi in front of my aunt's house where I stay during the week to go to school.

■ I have my own bedroom in my aunt's house.

■ This is my aunt Semaledene's dinner table where I do my homework.

■ My aunt's mother lives next to her in this house. These cousins wanted to be in the picture.

■ The kitchen in the house of my aunt. We use a coal stove to keep us warm in winter and to cook the Sunday lunch.

■ Pulani, my cousin, has just woken up in her bed on the floor. In winter it gets very cold and babies need lots of blankets.

■ Teacher Barotho who teaches from Grade 1 to Grade 3 in the garden of Thabiso Primary School.

■ Our school is on Smaldeel farm. This is the way to school. All the roads on the farm are dirt roads.

■ At my school they teach us six subjects. This is our English class and we are doing a writing exercise.

My school

Our school, Thabiso Primary School, is a farm-school. It ends with Grade 6. There are two classrooms. The first classroom is for Grade 1, Grade 2, Grade 3 and Grade 4. The second classroom is for Grade 5 and Grade 6. We have only two teachers, being Teacher Barotho and Teacher Mokoena. Teacher Mokoena comes from Koppies about 25 km away.

Our school starts at eight in the morning and closes at half past one. The school was started by Mr Dirkie Serfontein who lives on the next farm, Smaldeel. My first school on Mr Leonard's farm, Kristalkop, has closed down because there were not enough children. That is why I am studying at Thabiso and why my sister Mashease and I are staying at Smaldeel with our aunt Semaledene. There there are ten of us living with her.

Here they teach us Sesotho, English, Geography, History, Maths and Science. Of all the subjects I like Sesotho, English and Maths best.

■ This is our vegetable garden at school where we grow onions, carrots cabbage and beetroot which we eat at our school during break.

■ Make and Mpuse are in my class. They are posing in front of the blackboard during break.

■ My friends Ndade and Pisoso at school.

■ My friends and I are playing soccer on the soccer field.

■ Thabo, Pisoso and Sefako posing for a picture next to the soccer field.

■ Nzimene and Pisoso reading the newspaper with the national soccer results.

■ Pisoso outside his house. His brother is chopping wood.

■ My aunt is cooking in the black pot and my cousin is doing the washing in the zinc bath.

■ I shot a picture of these pigs because I like them so much. In my language you say: 'Fariki ena ke e shutile hoba ke e rata haholo'.

71

Fernando Luwango

The San were the first people to inhabit Southern Africa, but now they are a minority group who live almost everywhere in very difficult circumstances. Before fences were put up around the farms on which white farmers settled, the San were hunters and gatherers. They lived in the dry western part of Southern Africa and roamed far and wide, following game and collecting bulbs and berries, honey and other wild plants. For meat, they shot antelope such as gemsbok and springbok with bows and poisoned arrows. They knew how to live in dry, desert places and where to find water under the ground by digging. If there was no water, they tapped moisture from wild bulbs.

Schmidtsdrift was built on a South African Defence Force (SADF) base near Douglas in 1990. This town of tents was put up to give a temporary home to about 6 000 San people. Most of them were moved here from northern Namibia after the liberation war on the Angolan border was ended. Many were soldiers during the war, so when Namibia got its independence they had no work or place to stay.

The people of Schmidtsdrift were promised permanent houses in 1990, but they are still living in tents. The children go to school in corrugated iron structures, where in summer the temperature can go up to 42 degrees. When it is so hot, or when there is a heavy sand- or rainstorm, the school must be dismissed because conditions get too bad.

The San at Schmidtsdrift speak the ancient languages of !Xhu and Khwe at home, but at school the children are taught in Afrikaans and English.

FeRnando

I was born on 10 June, but I can't remember what year. I am twelve years old. I stay with my grandmother in a tent near the road. My grandfather did not like us so he took another wife and moved in with her. There is nobody who looks after me and my grandmother. My brother and sister left with my mother who works on a farm. My brother is called Julius. My sister later died. I do not know my father, I think he is in Namibia.

Nellie is my friend. She is older than I and we do things together.

I like watching TV, but we don't have one at home. I also like to play with my friends Semba and Chwenda. Fighting I like the least and of everything I'm most scared of a snake. Of all the kinds of food I like chicken and meat best.

Sundays my grandmother and I go to the Dutch Reformed church. When I'm big I want to be a teacher.

■ Our house. The tent in which my grandmother and I live. An old man has asked for water. We store our water in the green drum.

■ The grass near the tents in Schmidtsdrift after the rain. The grass and the soil are wet. It doesn't often rain.

■ My grandmother prepares food in our kitchen.

■ My friends are sitting in the kitchen. We are going to eat Grandma's food.

■ My friend Nellie took a picture of me where I'm still lying in bed before I got up to go to school.

■ I got up and first washed my face. After that I washed my whole body. Then we drank coffee and went to school.

■ I'm looking for clothes in the trunk to put on to go to school. I keep my clothes in the trunk.

■ Nellie next to the aloe which grows behind Mr Jonkers's office. Mr Jonkers is the principal of our school.

■ In the Maths and Science class. We are busy doing a task in our scribblers.

My school

The name of my school is Schmidtsdrift San Combined School and Mr Jonkers is the principal. Miss Amanda du Toit, who stays at Douglas, taught me how to read and write.

There are 1 200 learners in my school. I am in Grade 4B. We are 40 learners in Grade 4B. Most of the learners live in tents. Only about 50 come from Ou Schmidtsdrift.

They have always lived here. Their parents work in the SAMI (South African Military Institute).

I like going to school. School is enjoyable for me and I want to pass matric. Then I, too, want to teach learners.

In school we learn Afrikaans and English. Our school starts at quarter past seven in the morning because it gets very hot during the day. We go home at quarter past two. The school sometimes receives money for the feeding scheme and then we get food during break.

■ We used to get food at school. Here Marianna is busy mixing and preparing the food.

■ Bernanda, one of our cooks, and Rave, the caretaker, carry a pot of food to where it will be dished up.

■ Our school waiting at the cooking pots while Miss Marita hands out food to the learners. One of the Grade 2 learners stirs the food.

■ The small ones always sit down under the tree to eat. They get their food before the other learners, so they are not allowed to run around until the cook has rung the bell for break.

■ When we arrived at school everything was soaking wet. It had rained that much. Miss Nel let us carry all the benches outside so that they could dry off. We had our classes outside.

■ For the last two periods every Friday, we, the Grade 4s, watch videos in the video room.

■ The girls are doing traditional dances during break. They clap their hands and sing while they dance.

■ On 6 April our school closed for the Easter holidays until 18 April. All the learners went to the hall to receive their reports. I thought I had done well.

■ Miss Nel also gave all 40 learners in our class Easter eggs when the school closed. My friend Nellie and some other learners wait for their eggs.

■ The school bus, which brings the children from Ou Schmidtsdrift to school and takes them back again, is always parked at the SAMI.

■ I took a picture of the teachers' toilets because they look like strange things to me, things I have never seen before. This toilet is broken.

■ Nellie drinking water from a tap near the school. We don't have running water in our tents. There are about 20 taps in Schmidtsdrift.

■ Two friends who filled a pail of water from the tap are carrying it back to their tent.

■ These women pick the katollo ('suurgoed') which they had planted and then they put it in the sun to dry. When it has dried out, it gets cooked with some meat.

■ At Schmidtsdrift not much happens. Sala and another little girl fought with each other at the tents, because the other little girl teased Sala.

■ The baby is crying because her mother wanted someone else to hold her and she wanted her mother. The mother wanted to go and wash the baby's nappies.

Umir Misbach

Cape Town is one of the most beautiful cities in the world. It nestles at the foot of Table Mountain, with Devil's Peak on its left and Lion's Head and Signal Hill on its right. When the famous English navigator, Sir Francis Drake, sailed around the Cape on his sea journey around the world in 1580, he wrote in his diary: 'This cape is the fairest cape that we saw in all our circumference of the world.'

South Africa's written history started here when Commander Jan van Riebeeck landed at Table Bay in 1652. He and his small group of Dutch compatriots were sent by the Dutch East India Company (VOIC) to establish a refreshment station. The Cape lies halfway on the sea route between Europe and the East, so they had to supply fresh vegetables and meat to the trade ships of the VOIC on their way to and from Indonesia.

Cape Town has always been a cosmopolitan city. One group of people who have added a great deal to the character and culture and culinary art of the city are the Cape Malays. They were brought here by the VOIC as highly skilled slaves and political exiles. When these craftsmen and their families were freed, they settled above the city in the Bo-Kaap. Their descendants still live here.

Most of them belong to the Muslim faith.

Cape Town is the capital of the Western Cape. It is also the legislative capital of South Africa. The Houses of Parliament, where the laws are passed, are here. The MPs stay here only half the year because Pretoria is the administrative capital.

umiR

I was born on 30 August 1989 at Somerset Hospital in Cape Town. My mom says I was a very big baby.

We live in Bo-Kaap and our house is situated on the slopes of Signal Hill. It is a three-bedroomed house. I have been living here since I was born. I share a room with my brother. My father's par-

ents are our neighbours and my mother's parents live in Walmer Estate, not very far from us.

I love playing soccer, but I dislike having to get up early. My favourite food is McDonald's.

My biggest wish is to become a racing-car driver. I would love to travel the world.

■ This is my father Rushdie who has a carpentry business.

■ Our house is built on the slopes of Signal Hill and overlooks Cape Town.

■ From our house we have a wonderful view of Table Mountain. My mother is sitting in the lounge upstairs.

My family

There are four children in our family. My sister Fuzlin is the eldest. She is 22 years old. Then comes my brother Yusuf. He is 19 years old. My other sister Faiza is 16. I am the youngest and only 11 years old.

My father's name is Rushdie and he is a carpenter. My mother's name is Shaheeda and she owns a catering service in Woodstock called Shaheeda's Corporate Catering. Fuzlin works at Permanent Bank. Yusuf is still studying electronics. Faiza is in Grade 10 at Sea Point High School. It is an ordinary government school.

The most important people in my life are my parents.

We are a very close family and we always enjoy family get-togethers.

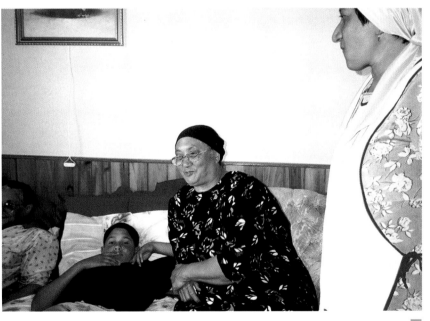

■ In the living room there is a 'rakam' which has the 99 names of Allah, our God.

■ My sister Faiza with Zubair, my cousin's baby who is practically our baby too.

■ My mother's aunts talking with my granny.

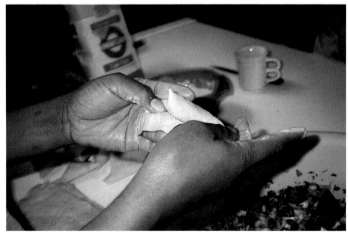

■ My mom's catering business specialises in Malay food, such as samoosas.

■ My father produces furniture, mainly cupboards, in his carpentry workshop. Here he is working in our yard.

■ With these spices, mixed with onion, tomato and coriander, we make vegetarian samoosas. We eat some almost every day.

■ A domestic helper preparing samoosas – a savoury usually filled with curried mince, chicken or vegetables.

■ When my granny came back from Mecca we had all sorts of luxuries, such as sweets, chips and mebos – a type of sweet made from apricots.

■ All Muslim people want to go on a pilgrimage to Mecca in Saudi Arabia at least once in their life time.

■ My grandmother went this year. My grandfather was very emotional when he welcomed her back.

■ The day after she returned the whole family came to visit her. Later that evening the women did their prayers.

■ This is the way to school. The road is very steep and walking back is hard.

■ My Islamic Studies teacher marking the pupils' homework.

■ Pupils in the school grounds before school starts. School begins at eight in the morning.

■ My class-mates playing cards on the last day of the school term.

My school

I attend Schotche Kloof Primary School which is situated in the Malay area of Bo-Kaap. My school is about five minutes' walk from our house. The principal's name is Mrs Dramat and my class teacher's name is Mr Ebrahim. I am in Grade 6. My best friend is Zayed Rylands.

It is a strictly Muslim school. We do normal school work as well as Islamic Studies. The founders of the Schotche Kloof were Dr Abdurahman and Sissy Gool who were Muslim community leaders. The school is about 50 years old.

■ I always have to polish my shoes the evening before. I spend about half an hour to get them to shine to my satisfaction.

■ I am in my room, preparing for mosque. I don't go every Friday though.

■ In the summer it gets very hot in Cape Town. This day it was so hot that even Fahier dared to take off his shirt so he could flex his muscles (fat) for us.

89

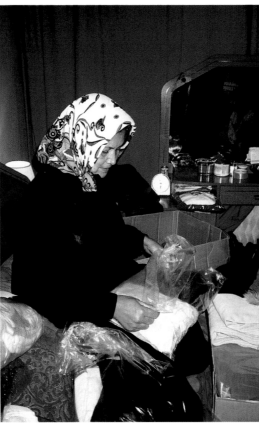

■ My sister Fuzlin got married to Hashim in April. Here the imam performs the marriage, the 'nikah', and tells the groom what his responsibilities are.

■ To seal the marriage, the groom has to give the dowry, the 'maskawi', to the imam to pass on to the bride's father.

■ Fuzlin was very nervous while my mom helped her to pack her clothes before moving to her new home.

■ Some wedding pictures were taken at Green Point next to the sea.

■ My sister on the night of her wedding at her new home.

■ The page-boy, Taurik, my father's cousin's grandchild. A page boy is the flower girl's partner.

■ My newly-married sister and brother-in-law Hashim entering the reception at Temple Hall, Green Point.

91

Natasha Sevan

Genadendal was the first mission station in South Africa. By 1737 already, only 85 years after the VOIC started a refreshment station at the Cape, a German by the name of Georg Schmidt settled here. He wanted to convert the Khoikhoi people in the area to Christianity. After five years he left. The Moravian Missionary Society for whom he worked did not want him to baptise his converts because he was not ordained as a minister. But in 1806, the same year the British took over the Cape, the Moravians returned. This time the mission effort was successful. A big church was built as well as a manse for the German missionary and white-washed cottages with black thatched roofs for the local people. A watermill was also erected and soon the small town of Genadendal – 'Valley of Grace' – thrived.

Genadendal is 120 km to the east of Cape Town. It is no longer a mission station, but the first Moravian church is still the biggest and most important building in the village. The central part is now a historic monument. In recent times two schools were built nearby: the L R Schmidt Primary School, named after the founder of the town, and the Emil Weder Senior Secondary School. There are also centres for adult and preschool education. Genadendal has about 6 000 inhabitants. The four educational institutions teach more than 1 300 learners. Some learners come from far away and are at boarding school.

In 1995 former President Mandela gave the official Cape Town residence of the President a new name. It is now called Genadendal.

NatasHa

I was born in 2 Military Hospital in Wynberg, Cape Town, on 20 December 1989. At the age of three, my sister and I moved to Genadendal to stay with my grandmother. My parents remained behind to work, my father at the South Africa Navy in Simon's Town and my mother at OK Bazaars.

My hobbies are cycling and swimming. I also like house parties and solo singing at school. I am a member of our Moravian Church's junior choir, as well as member of the Kinderbond youth club.

I've already been crowned Miss Valentine and Miss ElektroWise. I was also second princess in the Miss L R Schmidt competition in which my sister was crowned queen.

I have a little dog by the name of Misty. When I come home from school, he meets me halfway. Sometimes I want to crunch him to death I like him so much! My favourite food is macaroni-cheese. I also like eating out. For my birthday we usually eat at the Spur steakhouse.

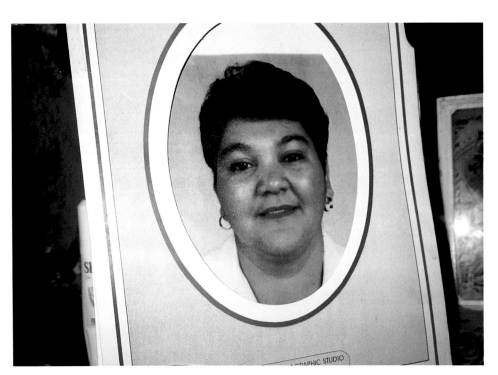

■ We live in Berg Street. Here Jessica and Suzette are in my street. In the background you can see Grootkop. Genadendal lies amongst mountains.

■ My dad has to get up at 5 in the morning to work in the bakery. He always take a nap in the afternoon. Here he is asleep on the sofa in our TV room, with Suné next to him.

■ A photograph of my mother Desirine who died in 1999.

My family

I lost my mother when I was nine. Her name was Desirine. That was the greatest sadness in my short life. I miss her very much, but we regularly put fresh flowers on her grave. There is a new woman, Suné, in my father's life who looks after us and does her best to make life easier for us. I have an older sister, Nicole, who is 14, and a little brother or sister on the way. I also have three grandmothers.

My dad Ivan now works full-time at the bakery here in Genadendal. We have been living where we now live for 10 months. The house has a big kitchen, a pantry, a lounge, a dining room, four bedrooms, two bathrooms, a toilet, wash room, study and a leisure room.

My sister stays in Caledon with my aunty Nicole, who runs a hairsalon, because she doesn't like Genadendal.

The thing I like least is washing and drying dishes.

■ I'm standing between the wardrobe and the dressing table in my room. Every time I open the door, I see my mom, because there is a picture of her pasted on the inside.

■ My sister Nicole in her room. She is 14 and is crazy about film stars and pop singers.

■ Our kitchen. We always eat here. Sometimes I do the dishes.

■ My sister and I let the bath overflow and had to dry the bathroom. Sometimes we give my father grey hairs because we don't want to do the chores in the house.

■ My girlfriends and I like dressing up as film stars and models.

■ Olga, Magdelena, Rachê, Jennelee and Lelanie sitting together on the sofa in Jennelee's house. She is my best friend and stays nextdoor to us.

■ I have a stocking on my head, even though I don't need to straighten my hair by walking around and sleeping with it on my head.

■ For fun we sometimes do break-dancing in the street in the evening. There are not many cars in Genadendal, so one can safely play in the street.

■ We all walk to school in the mornings. It takes about ten minutes. The town is spread out on both sides of the stream that runs past the school. We walk to school through the old part of town.

■ Each Friday during Art and Culture class we have to clean the environment for an hour. Every bit of litter is put in big bags.

■ Some children bring their own sandwiches to school and those who can't afford it always get something to eat at school.

My school

At age six I went to L R Schmidt Primary School's pre-primary and the next year my real school career started at the same school where I'm now in Grade 6. My teacher's name is Mr Mackenzie. He lives at Caledon. Every day he travels 40 km to Genadendal. There are 30 children in my class. There are 537 children in my school and there are 15 teachers.

I have many friends at school. We speak Afrikaans. Our school starts at eight in the morning and closes at two. At quarter to ten we have a break and at quarter past twelve we have second break. During first break we eat sandwiches, during second break I always play.

I'm member of the school choir and the drum majorettes as well as the student council. At the moment I'm playing Cinderella in the our school operetta. I regularly support our school activities.

■ In Grade 6 we do computer lessons only in summer. In Grade 7 we will work more regularly on computers.

■ This is my class, Grade 6A. We are 30 in my class.

■ I sing in the school choir on Tuesdays and Thursdays. Mr Balie, who teaches us Afrikaans and Life Skills, is also our choirmaster.

■ The Genadendal Junior Choir regularly practise in the original Moravian church in the middle of town. I also sing in this choir, sometimes even solo.

■ The two donkeys in our town are famous. They always wander around the old part of town.

■ This is Violet. The name of the other donkey, on the photo opposite, is Muffin.

■ Children playing with sticks and tires.

■ Warren Mills

Grahamstown was started as a military outpost by the British in 1812, to try to keep the peace on the eastern border of the Cape Colony. The Fish River, about 40 km away, was the official border. On the other side the Xhosa people lived.

Soon the struggling little outpost became a proper town. In 1820 the British Settlers arrived. They were given land in the border area and started to farm, build houses and hunt. But soon many of them left their farms and came to Grahamstown instead, to earn a living by using the skills they had learnt in Britain. Within a few years the town had the second largest number of millers, carpenters, wheelwrights, blacksmiths and gunsmiths in the whole country. Only Cape Town had more and was bigger.

Today Grahamstown is just a small city. It is known as 'city of the saints' and 'the city of schools'. This is because it boasts 40 places of worship – even a cathedral – and some of the best schools in South Africa, many of them boarding schools. The famous Rhodes University is also in Grahamstown.

Despite the many learners and students, Grahamstown is a quiet, out of the way place - except in July, when visitors arrive in huge numbers for the National Arts Festival. This annual cultural event was started 20 years ago.

The capital of the Eastern Cape is Bishu, about 115 km north of Grahamstown. In this whole area agriculture is very important. The farmers produce wool and meat, and the most delicious pineapples. There are also wonderful game reserves.

WaRren

I was born on 20 June 1991 at Settlers Hospital in Grahamstown. The earliest thing I can remember is playing with my first dog, Buster the bulldog.

I have a big ox called Tora now and I like riding him. My favourite horse is Viking. My other pets are Madusa the snake and Timon the meerkat. Timon sleeps with me in my bed. Before, Pumba my little warthog also slept on my bed, but Pumba is with Jesus now and I miss him.

What I like doing most is drawing lots of pictures. And what I like least is cleaning up the animals' poo.

When I'm big I want to be a game ranger with an aeroplane to watch my animals from the sky, and also a jeep and my horse. I also hope I can get enough money to take my family to see America.

■ My mom and brother Steven are shooting bow and arrow in front of our house at Donkerbosch Outspan.

■ Here Mom is making grass targets for her archery.

■ Every morning we all have breakfast in the kitchen. Then Mom or Dad takes us to school in town.

My family

My family loves animals. We live on a farm at Stoneshill near Grahamstown. The name of the farm is Donkerbosch Outspan, which means 'the dark forest where wagons camp'.

My brother Steven is eight years old and he is always feeding his rabbits. My mommy has very long golden hair. She loves her horses and trains them. She also loves Merlin the owl. Mommy works at the Settlers' Monument in Grahamstown. My dad is a farmer and an outreach education officer at the museum in Grahamstown and game parks in the area. He takes lots of children to bush camps and teaches them about nature. Daddy loves history and animals.

Our house is so big that an elephant can sleep in it and my horse can come inside.

■ Daddy is taking Pumba, my warthog, for a ride in his Buffalo Bill bakkie. I am very sad because Pumba died a short time after I took this picture.

■ My meerkat Timon and Pumba the warthog used to sleep with me in my bed.

■ My brother Steven likes to read his dinosaur book before he goes to sleep.

■ The people who work on our farm also stay here with their families. Nosophe and her child collect fire wood from the forest to use in their stove.

■ On our farm we prefer to use animals instead of machines. Fezile and Nqanqa are ploughing the field using oxen and a hand-held plough.

■ Here my dad is dipping the cattle to get rid of the ticks on them. Mzile, one of our workers, is helping him.

■ Uncle John Sneyd grows proteas, our national flower. Here he gives Mommy a big bunch.

■ We have a dam behind our house where we swim when it is hot.

■ Grandpa also has a dam on his farm. Here Grandpa and I catch fish in his dam.

■ I go to Oatlands Preparatory School. During break we sometimes stay in our classroom.

■ My teacher, Mrs Nel.

■ Our new South African flag.

My school

The name of my school is Oatlands Preparatory School. It is 52 years old. The headmistress is Mrs Walwyn and my class teacher is Mrs Nel. She has long black hair and she is very kind to us.

There are lots of children in my school. My school has a library, an art room and a nice playground. It goes up to Grade 3. Mrs Nel teaches us Sums, History and Afrikaans. Mrs Holiday does Xhosa with us.

We have a sports field were we play soccer, cricket and hockey and running sports. My school colours are blue.

■ We do different sports at my school. Here we practise cricket.

■ I am a member of the Cub Scouts. We meet every Friday afternoon after five. Here my Wolf Pack is having a braai.

■ Sometimes my dad arranges rides by ox wagon. Here my class is going to our farm house.

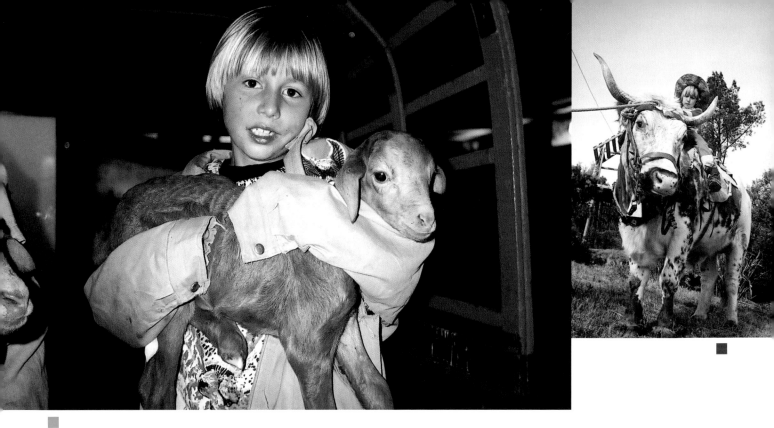

■ Steven also loves animals. This is a baby goat he is holding.

■ I love my pet ox Tora. Not many people ride on oxen, but in my family we do. We have specially trained Tora to carry people.

■ There is still a lot of wildlife in the mountains where we live. Our family often looks after hurt animals. Here my mother's sister, Aunt Geraldine, takes care of a baby kudu in her house.

■ My dad is telling the story of the dung beetle to a group of school children. He is an education officer at the museum and game parks and knows a lot about nature.

■ A dung beetle pushing a ball of dung which he has cut and rolled out of a cow patty.

■ Ken and Welcome are game rangers. Here they are on our farm with Dad and Monty the python.

■ We have a hiking group. Here my dad is leading us up Buffelskop in the Cradock district in the Karoo to see Olive Schreiner's grave on top of the mountain. Olive Schreiner was a writer.

■ Avanthi Singh

Durban, KwaZulu-Natal

Durban is the biggest city in the province of KwaZulu-Natal. It is also one of Africa's most important harbour cities, handling large volumes of import and export goods. Sugar is its most important agricultural cargo. About 24 million tons of sugarcane are cut and refined into sugar each year. A large portion of this is exported to places all over the world.

Sugarcane, which is grown throughout the province, is the reason why Durban has such a large Indian community. When sugar production was started about 150 years ago, experienced people were needed to work in the cane fields. To solve the problem, the British, who governed Natal, decided to recruit people from India.

So from 1860 onwards thousands of Indians were brought to Durban by ship. For the first five years these 'indentured' immigrants were not free. They worked for their food, clothing and accommodation and very little pay. But when their contracts were finished, they could return to India or stay. Many did not go back but made the new country their home and settled in Durban. Today many of them have become very successful business people.

KwaZulu-Natal stretches from Mozambique in the north to the Eastern Cape in the south. All along the Indian Ocean coast line there are wonderful beaches, but Durban is the most popular holiday resort by far. It has a warm subtropical climate and large numbers of holiday-makers from elsewhere in the country visit Durban during the cold winter months of June and July. Others prefer to come at Christmas time, even though it gets unpleasantly hot and humid in summer.

Avanthi

I was born on 26 June 1991 in St Augustus Hospital in Musgrave, Durban. We have been living in the same house since my birth. Our house is very big with a thatched roof and eight bedrooms. It is in Westville.

I love playing with my dog because he is cute, energetic and loving. My best friends are Dahna Johnson, Nandi Mbatha, Bhavika Khoosal, Mayuri Ravjee – and my whole class at school. In the picture above, I am on the left and Bhavika is on the right.

I go to church and to the temple. I like to pray.

I do not quite know yet what I want to do when I am grown up, but I'm thinking of one of three choices: to be model, an actress or fashion designer. Or a photographer!

■ My beautiful house. It is huge and has a thatched roof like the houses in the Cape. Inside it is nice and warm and cosy. I have lived in this house for as long as I can remember.

■ My mom is all dressed up to go somewhere. She is sitting in my parents' bedroom, her favourite spot, where she also does most of her studying. I like the way my mom dresses.

■ This old teapot has been in my mom's family for a long time. It stands in our lounge where we receive our visitors. I like this room because it carries lots of family memories and some family photos.

My family

At the moment there are six people altogether living in our house: my granny and my two cousins Babu and Naadiah. They are brother and sister and come from Canada. And then there are my parents and me. I have one brother, one sister and another sister who is a presenter on TV. They are much older than me and do not live at home any more.

I like my family. We have dinners together and we always have fun. My family spans three generations, and my granny is a great-grandmother to 13 children. Some of my family live very near us, but some live overseas.

My father used to have clothing factories in England and South Africa, but now he is retired. My mom is a speech and drama teacher and teaches from home. But she also studies and teaches English at the University of Natal.

■ This is my mom. She is studying because she has gone back to university this year. She enjoys reading.

■ My dad watches a lot of television because he sold his businesses and is retired.

■ This is Gertrude. She has been working for our family since I was a baby. She speaks Zulu and during weekends she visits her family in Hammersdale 35km away.

■ My granny from my father's side lives in Johannesburg, but during winter she comes to live with us because it is too cold in Gauteng then. It never gets very cold in Durban. Granny is 93 years old and very strong for her age.

■ My other granny, my mom's mother, lives in Durban. I call her Nani.

■ My aunt Lallen and my cousin Naadiah's Granny Goolab. Naadiah's granny passed away recently. The funeral was a sad affair because Naadiah's uncle Vijay, Granny Goolab's son, died shortly before.

■ Here Naadiah prepares to go to her granny's funeral.

■ There are many different religions in Durban. Here a new Hindu temple is opened and devotees honour their gods by carrying them through the streets in a parade.

■ My friend's neighbours in Durban moved out of their house. Before they left they needed five girls to pray and to eat some food which was specially prepared. In their Tamil culture they believe that little girls are like little princesses.

■ My school, the School of New Jerusalem, is a private school. Only 80 children go there.

■ James Guthrie, who also attends my school, standing in front of the school church. We have a service here every morning before our other lessons start.

■ All the pupils are taken to school by car. The parents take turns to do the driving. Here I have just been dropped off at the front entrance of the school.

My school

In my school there are eight teachers. It is called the School of New Jerusalem. Mr Buss is our principal. All the teachers are very nice.

It is a Christian school and we are Hindu, but I like going there because I like to learn about different religions. My favourite subject is Writing Workshop. In Writing Workshop we write our own plays and then act them out. I also like Art. In the afternoons we play hockey, cricket, swimming and other sports at school.

My best friends are Mayuri, Bhavika and Nandi. It's a very happy school where the teachers and the parents and the children get together for fun occasions.

■ Afrikaans lessons with Mrs Mitchell. We are doing work sheets on our Easter holidays. Mrs Mitchell also teaches us Zulu. At school I take three languages – English as my first language, Afrikaans and Zulu.

■ The Zulu session. We don't just learn the language. We also learn about the culture and here we play with some 'teaching aids'.

■ Reshni, Rebecca, Candice, Chelsie, Tayne, S'lindile and Megan are in different grades but they are all my friends. Here they are chatting on the sports field during first break.

■ My two best friends, Nandi and Mayuri, often go home with me in the afternoons because we do some school projects together. Bhavika, my other best friend, shares my portrait on page 113 with me.

■ These are Indian pickles made with lemon and mango.

■ My mom is always cooking and trying to please us with food. But the kitchen is not her favourite spot. I like the food she makes, especially the traditional Indian dishes.

■ Dogs are not welcome in our kitchen and my beloved Spotty and Patch always stayed outside. Patch died a few weeks after this picture was taken.

■ This soup is called 'cadhi'. It is served with plain rice. It is made with natural yoghurt and spices. My granny often cooks this soup.

■ Roti is made with flour and boiling water and is fried like a pancake.

■ Sun City in Northwest, where we spend our Easter holidays. It took us five hours to drive here from Durban. Sun City is a famous tourist destination. They call this the Valley of the Waves. Actually it is an artificial sea in the middle of nowhere. What fascinates me is that the waves here are sometime bigger than sea waves.

■ On the last day my dad took us to the crocodile farm. There are about 120 crocodiles. They all seemed asleep.

Mlungesi Ntuli

Ulundi is the capital of KwaZulu-Natal. This province is called after the Zulu people who moved south from central Africa centuries ago and settled here – 'KwaZulu' means 'Place of the Zulu'. 'Natal' comes from the name Vasco da Gama, the famous Portuguese navigator, gave the area where Durban is today. He named it 'Rio de Natal' – 'River of the Nativity' – because he saw this stretch of coast, full of rivers and lagoons, for the first time on Christmas Day 1497.

The Zulus took their name, which means 'Heaven', from Dinizulu, their first great leader. The Zulus are famous warriors. After Dinizulu came the great warrior and king, Shaka. He built up a mighty army and nation, but he was killed by his half-brother Dingane. Dingane fought fierce battles against the whites who wanted to settle in Natal. He defeated the Voortrekkers, who came from the Cape, so they left. But it was not the end of the fighting. After Dingane, Cetswayo became the new Zulu king. He was the one who made Ulundi the capital of the Zulu people in 1873. Then it was called 'uluNdi' – 'The Heights'. Next, the British wanted to have Natal. Cetswayo won some battles, but in the end his impis – soldiers – were defeated by the British army and Natal become a British colony.

Cattle have always played a very important part in the Zulu way of life. Cow's milk makes up a large part of the diet and traditionally a man's wealth was measured by the number of cattle he owned. Cattle was also used to pay 'lobola' – the compensation a bridegroom paid his father-in-law for his bride.

Mlungesi

I was born on 11 November 1988 in Durban, but I never lived there.

I'm a soccer player, like my brothers. I have already won three medals and one trophy. Now I am a member of the under-14 selection of the KwaZulu-Natal soccer team. My best friend is Sizwe. He plays in my team. My biggest wish is to play for Manchester United in England one day..

The most important person in my life is my mother because she gives me love and support. My worst fear is to be crashed down by a car. I'd like to be a doctor one day, because I'd like to save people's lives.

■ This is my house in Section D of Ulundi. It has eight rooms. I share this house with many people: my mother, my aunt, three brothers and one cousin.

■ My mother was relaxing in the lounge when I came home from school. My mother is a shy person.

■ Ulundi Section D. I tried to take a picture of the neighbourhood from the roof of my house. I like Section D because it is in a peaceful section.

My family

We live in Ulundi Section D in KwaZulu-Natal. We are ten in my family. There is my grandfather, grandmother, mother, cousin, four brothers, myself and my aunt. We have been living here for 13 years. My dad's mother and father live in Durban at KwaMashu Township. The mother of my mother lives near us at Manekwane, the next village after Mahlabathini, which is part of Ulundi.

My mother is the only person in my family who works. She is a nurse and works at the Health Department in Ulundi. My father had a tuck shop, but he died in a car accident in 1995.

We all like to watch and play sport, especially soccer. We enjoy staying together and making jokes. We laugh a lot. My wish for my family is that we will one day stay in Cape Town.

■ My mother is a nurse. She has decided to study further to get a higher position so that she can get a pay increase. She studies very hard.

■ My bother Minenhle is cheering his favourite soccer team, Mamelodi Sundowns from Pretoria.

■ My brother Syabonga is 20 years old. He finished school four years ago. Now he is studying at a techikon in Gauteng. He is a very peaceful and happy boy, who likes to play soccer and to sleep a lot.

■ My bother Xolani is 16 years old and in Grade 8. He has been practising karate for three years.

■ Our other home is at Manekwane, the next village after Mahlabathini, where my mother's mother stays. This is the kitchen hut.

■ Grandma Gogo is fetching water with her grandchild Sibusisiwe at Manekwane. My grandmother always gives me sweets when she sees me.

■ This is my grandfather, my mother's father, and his friend Mahaye. They were coming from the tavern and then they are always very funny.

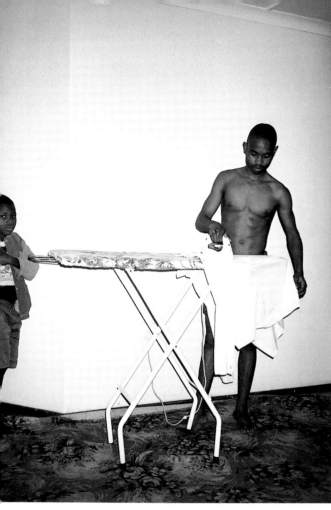

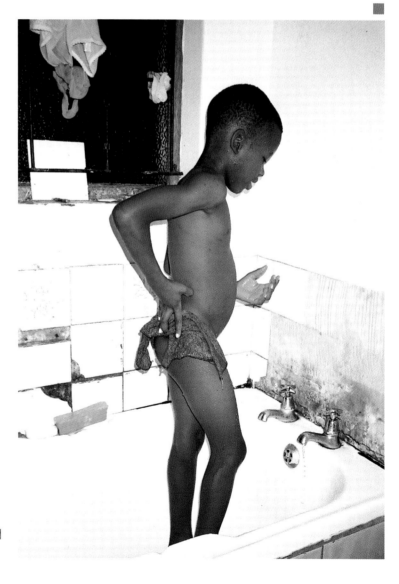

■ Xolani has to do the ironing on Sundays. He is ironing his school shirt which is part of his school uniform. School uniforms are of number one importance.

■ Soccer is our favourite sport. Everyone of us plays it. Even Khayelihle is playing with his friends Vuyo and Siyo.

■ My cousin Khayelihle is taking a bath before bedtime. He is nine and in Grade 2 and lives with us.

■ These children at my school are trained by the traffic police to help us cross the road when we come to school in the mornings and leave in the afternoons. Since I started going to school no one has ever been hit by a car.

■ Miss Suga Mhlongo, my class teacher, just loves to talk!

■ The boys in my class at morning assembly. The boys and the girls line up separately.

My school

The name of my school is Mahlabathini Public Primary School. It is in the Sishwili Mahlabathini district, about 10 km from Ulundi. The principal of my school is Mr Msimango. Altogether there are 35 teachers in my school. My school starts from Grade 3 and goes up to Grade 7. I am doing grade 7B. We are 76 in my class.

My class teacher is Miss Gugu Suga Mhlongo. I like to go to school because it gives me a future. My success depends on my schooling.

The motto of our school is 'Sebenza Uthan-daze'. In English it means: Work and Pray. I believe in prayer because when you pray Jesus makes your thoughts pure.

■ My class-mates at the river next to the school. We were taught about aquatic animals such as frogs and fish and about the environment. We completed the project successfully and afterwards we had a braai to celebrate it.

■ During second break these women sell us food. They bring fruit, vetkoek, Simba chips and hot chips, my favourite.

■ Every day after school my class-mate Thabiso has to collect the family cattle on his way home.

■ This ox had a broken leg. It owners later came to fetch it to slaughter it at their place.

■ Cattle are very important where we live. This is a cattle kraal. The cows are brought here before they are milked.

■ My uncle, who came to visit, eating cooked meat from the pot. The meat on the table was bought from the butcher and was not slaughtered by us.

■ Our local store in Section C and D. It used to be a sea container. We use it a lot because you can buy everything you need there. The first picture shows the inside, the second one the outside.

■ We still have many traditional houses with thatched roofs in Ulundi, such as the kitchen at Manekwane on page 126. This lady is cutting grass near town to fix her roof.

■ Our neighbour, MaCebekhulu, is plaiting grass. It looks like she is going to make a grass mat for the door.

Acknowledgements

The author dedicates this book to Pearl, Yannick, Joop and Lotte Lans for their support and trust.

Sincere thanks to the following organisations and individuals who through their financial support made the publication of this book possible:

Beith Photolab, Johannesburg;
B J's Photolab, Cape Town;
Han Lans Amsterdam bv;
ICE Models, Cape Town;
Nationale Commissie voor Duurzame Ontwikkeling, NCDO;
Dutch Embassy in South Africa;
Stichting Novib;
Fonds Verenigde Spaarbank, VSB Fonds.

The author also wishes to express his gratitude to:

Annari van der Merwe, who found the children and made the book possible;
Carl Niehaus, for his support and trust when the book was only an idea still;
Sonja Nijon of Contra Corrente, for her assistance with raising funds;
Steffi Freier of ICE Models, my first sponsor;
Stichting Kinderpostzegels for supporting the South African publication of the book;
Luwazi Mashaka, Seipati Mokheti and Sello Molefe of Emzansi for their assistance, guidance and translations of the isiXhosa and Sesotho texts.
France Productions, Cape Town, for all support and usage of their office.

As well as to all parents and teachers and other contact persons who gave of their time so generously and enthusiastically:

Tenda Madima, Daisy Nenguda and Mrs Makwarela; Ian Eversen and Letta and Morris Roda; Graeme Friedman, Carmit and Saul Bamberger and Mrs Steyn; Z B Molefe, Pinkie Khanyile, Mrs Banjwa and Thobeka Banjwa; Lyndal Erasmus and Nerine and John Leonard; Amanda du Toit; Shereen Misbach and Rushdie and Shaheeda Misbach; Ferdinand Hans and Ivan Sevan; Catherine Knox and Basil and Debbie Mills, Uma Meshtrie and Mr and Mrs Singh; Mr Mandla Msibi, Mr Msimango and Mrs Ntuli.

Designed by interactive.africa